Nobody Listens to Andrew

by Elizabeth Guilfoile

Follett Publishing Company

Chicago   New York

Library of Congress Catalog Card Number: 57-11019

NINTH PRINTING

Andrew saw something upstairs.

He ran down very fast.

He said,

    "Listen, Mother."

Mother said,

"Wait, Andrew.

I must pay Mrs. Cleaner.

She must catch the bus before dark."

Andrew said,

    "Listen, Daddy.

    I saw something upstairs."

Daddy said,

    "Wait, Andrew.

    I must cut the grass before dark."

Andrew said,

"Listen, Ruthy.

I saw something upstairs.

It was in my bed."

Ruthy said,

"Wait, Andrew.

I must put on my roller skates.

I want to skate before dark."

Andrew said,

"Listen, Bobby.

I saw something upstairs.

It was in my bed on the sun porch."

Bobby said,

"Don't bother me, Andrew.

I must find my bat and ball.

I want to play ball before dark."

Andrew said,

"Listen, Mr. Neighbor.

I saw something upstairs.

It was in my bed on the sun porch.

It was black."

Mr. Neighbor said,

"Never mind, Andrew.

I must take my dog for a walk

before dark."

Andrew said very loud,

    "Listen, Mother,

    Listen, Daddy,

    Listen, Ruthy,

    Listen, Bobby,

    Listen, Mr. Neighbor,

    Listen, Mrs. Cleaner,

    THERE IS A BEAR UPSTAIRS

    IN MY BED."

Mother stopped paying Mrs. Cleaner.

She said, "Call the police!"

Daddy stopped cutting the grass.

He said, "Call the fire department!"

Bobby stopped playing ball.

He said, "Call the dog catcher!"

Ruthy stopped skating. She said,

"Call the zoo!"

Mr. Neighbor stopped taking his dog
for a walk.

He called the police.

He called the fire department.

He called the dog catcher.

He called the zoo.

"Zoom!" came the police.

"Zing!" came the fire department.

"Whoosh!" came the dog catcher.

"Swish!" came the man from the zoo.

They all ran upstairs.

"Look!" said Mother.

"It is on the sun porch."

"Look!" said Daddy. "It is black."

"Look!" said Bobby.

"It is on Andrew's bed."

"Look!" said Ruthy. "It is a bear.

Andrew said it was a bear.

But nobody listens to Andrew."

The dog catcher caught the bear
in his net.
The fireman said,
"It climbed up the tree.
It climbed in the window."

The man from the zoo said,
"It is dry in the woods.
The bears are thirsty.
They are looking for water.
I will take this bear to the zoo."

Daddy said,

"Next time we will listen to Andrew."

NOBODY LISTENS TO ANDREW

By Elizabeth Guilfoile

Reading Level: Level One. *Nobody Listens to Andrew* has a total vocabulary of 104 words. It has been tested in first grade classes, where the children read it with delight and were very unwilling to part with it.

Uses of this Book: This book is for fun. The triumph of the little boy who has something really important to say when his elders finally realize what he has been trying to tell them is very satisfying to young readers. The repetition of words and phrases that is so important for beginning readers is here an integral part of an exciting story, and various community helpers are introduced in a very natural way. Incidentally, this story is based on real events of one summer in Minnesota.

Word List

All of the 104 words used in *Nobody Listens to Andrew* are listed. Regular plurals (*-s*) and regular verb forms (*-s, -ed, -ing*) of words already on the list are not listed separately, but the endings are given in parenthesis after the word.

5	Andrew('s)		said		she
	saw		listen(s)		catch
	something		Mother		the
	upstairs	6	wait		bus
	he		I		before
	ran		must		dark
	down		pay(ing)	7	Daddy
	very		Mrs.		cut
	fast		Cleaner		grass

8 Ruthy
   it
   was
   in
   my
   bed
   put
   on
   roller
   skate(s)
   want
   to

9 Bobby
   sun
   porch

10 don't
   bother
   me
   find
   bat
   and
   ball
   play(ing)

11 Mr.
   Neighbor

   black
   never
   mind
   take
   dog
   for
   a
   walk

12 loud
   there
   is
   bear(s)

13 stopped
   call(ed)
   police
   cutting
   fire
   department

14 catcher
   skating
   zoo

15 taking
   his

17 zoom
   came

19 zing

20 whoosh
   swish
   man
   from

21 they
   all

22 look(ing)
   but
   nobody

24 caught
   net
   fireman
   climbed
   up
   tree
   window

25 dry
   woods
   are
   thirsty
   water
   will
   this

26 next
   time
   we

The Follett BEGINNING-TO-READ Books

Purpose of the Beginning-to-Read Books: To provide easy-to-read materials that will appeal to the interests of primary children. Careful attention is given to vocabulary load and sentence length, but the first criterion is interest to children.

Reading Levels: These books are written at three reading levels, indicated by one, two, or three dots beneath the *Beginning-to-Read* symbol on the back cover. *Level One* books can be read by first grade children in the last half of the school year. As children increase their reading ability they will be able to enjoy *Level Two* books. And as they grow further in their reading ability they will progress to *Level Three* books. Some first grade children will read *Level Two* and *Level Three* books. Many third graders, and even some fourth graders, will read and enjoy *Level One* and *Level Two* books, as well as *Level Three* books. The range of interest of *Beginning-to-Read* books stretches far beyond their reading level.

Use of the Beginning-to-Read Books: Because of their high interest and readability, these books are ideal for independent reading by primary children—at school, in the library, and at home. The books may also be incorporated into the basic reading program to develop children's interests, expand their vocabularies, and improve word-attack skills. It has been suggested that they might serve as the foundation for a skillfully directed reading program. Many *Beginning-to-Read* books correlate with the social studies, science, and other subject fields. All will help children grow in the language arts. Children will read the *Beginning-to-Read* books with confidence, with success, and with real enjoyment.